With love to Tom, Luke and Isaac,
and everyone who cares about nature.

Text and illustrations copyright © Petr Horáček 2019

First published in Great Britain in 2019 by
Otter-Barry Books, Little Orchard, Burley Gate,
Herefordshire, HR1 3QS
www.otterbarrybooks.com

A catalogue record for this book is available from the British Library.

ISBN 978-1-910959-71-8

Illustrated with mixed media

Set in Bembo

Printed in China

9 8 7 6 5 4 3 2 1

The Last
TIGER

Petr Horáček

Otter-Barry BOOKS

Deep in the jungle
lived a fearless tiger.
No other animal was as strong
and powerful as he was.

One day hunters came to the jungle.
All the animals tried to hide.
All except the tiger.

"You have to hide!"
the other animals warned him.

"I'm not scared," growled the tiger.
"I'm the strongest, most powerful animal
in the jungle."

Next day the hunters spotted the tiger. They had never seen such a magnificent creature before.

"Catching this tiger would make US the strongest and most powerful," they thought.

The hunters returned to the city
and made a cunning plan...

Then they returned to the jungle.
There were more of them now
and they brought nets.

Soon the tiger was overpowered and captured.

He was taken to the city
so that everyone could see him.

The tiger was kept in a cage.

People from far and wide
came to see him. They marvelled
at the big, strong tiger,
as he looked out at them
from behind the bars.

He was very unhappy.

In his dreams
the tiger ran
through the jungle.

Now, in captivity, he realised
that his strength and power meant
nothing any more.
What he longed for was freedom.

The tiger in the cage became sadder and weaker.

Soon people stopped coming to see him.

He was getting smaller every day.

And then it happened....

One night, the tiger realised that now
he could squeeze through the bars
of his cage.

And that's exactly what he did!

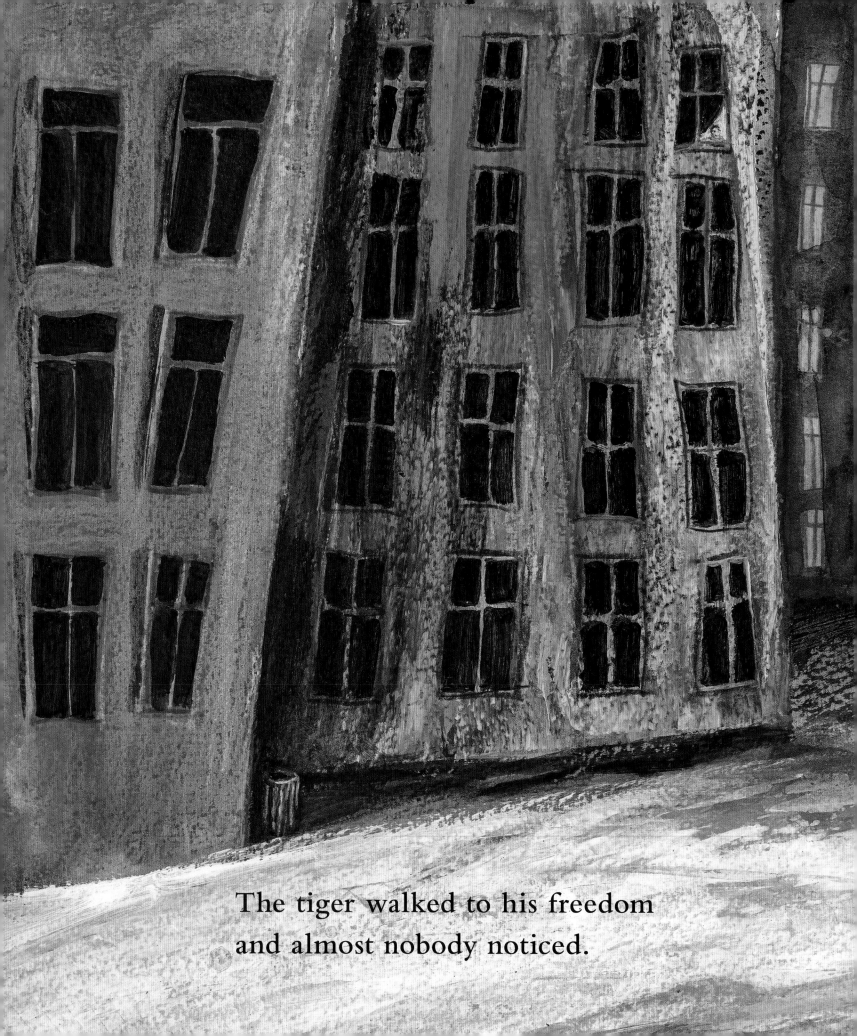

The tiger walked to his freedom
and almost nobody noticed.

In time the tiger became big and strong.
He made sure that no man would ever
see him again. And he never forgot
that his most treasured possession was
not his strength or his power...

it was his freedom.